For Poppy Rose, with love
~ M C B

For Kais Bahrani
~ T M

tiger tales
5 River Road, Suite 128, Wilton, CT 06897
Published in the United States 2013
Originally published in Great Britain 2013
by Little Tiger Press
Text copyright © 2013 M. Christina Butler
Illustrations copyright © 2013 Tina Macnaughton
ISBN-13: 978-1-58925-145-8 • ISBN-10: 1-58925-145-8
Printed in China • LTP/1800/0570/0613

For more insight and activities, visit us at www.tigertalesbooks.com

Library of Congress Cataloging-in-Publication Data

Butler, M. Christina.
 One special Christmas / by M. Christina Butler ; illustrated by Tina
Macnaughton.
    pages cm
"Originally published in Great Britain 2013."
 Summary: On Christmas Eve, Little Hedgehog is delighted to deliver some
presents for the ailing Santa, but he will never be able to finish the job
in time without help from his friends.
 ISBN 978-1-58925-145-8 (hardcover) — ISBN 1-58925-145-8 (hardcover) [1.
Christmas—Fiction. 2. Hedgehogs—Fiction. 3. Animals—Fiction.] I.
Macnaughton, Tina, illustrator. II. Title.
 PZ7.B97738Onb 2013
 [E]—dc23
                                    2013009284

One Special Christmas

by M. Christina Butler

Illustrated by Tina Macnaughton

tiger tales

It was Christmas Eve, and Little Hedgehog
was busy in his kitchen.

"*We wish you a merry Christmas!*" he sang,
stirring his yummy cake mixture.

Just then, something landed BUMP!
outside his window . . . .

It was a sled full of presents, with a note:
Dear Little Hedgehog, I have a terrible cold and
need your help! Would you be able to deliver these
Christmas presents for me? Thank you! Love, Santa.

"Oh, my!" squeaked Little Hedgehog, rushing to wrap up warmly. "Don't worry, Santa! I'm on my way!"

A big moon was shining in the dark sky as Little Hedgehog hurried up the hill to Mouse's house.

He squeezed
inside and tucked
three tiny presents under
the Christmas tree.
"Mouse and her babies
will be so excited!" he whispered.
"But I'd better be quick—there's
a lot more to deliver!"

With a big push,
Little Hedgehog jumped
onto the sled and zoomed
off, faster and faster
down the hill.

"Whee!" he laughed.
"I'm just like Santa!"

"What was that?" cried Rabbit,
as the sled sped past.

"It's Little Hedgehog!"
yelled Fox. "He's going
much too fast!"

Suddenly, the sled hit a snowdrift
with a BUMP! and flew up into
the air . . .

...CRASH!

"Little Hedgehog!" cried Rabbit and Fox, pulling him out of the snow.

"Thank you!" puffed Little Hedgehog. "But look— the presents are scattered everywhere! I have to deliver them for Santa!"

"We'll help," said Fox. "Great!" replied Little Hedgehog. "We can use my hat as a bag!"

So they tugged and
heaved, and they squashed
and squeezed . . .

until every last
present was in!

Laughing and giggling, they sped
off again.

"Santa's helpers are coming!"
cried Little Hedgehog.

But as they passed a holly bush, the
hat caught on the prickly leaves, and
the wool started to unravel . . . .

The hat got smaller and
smaller . . . and one by one,
the presents fell out!

"Oh no!" groaned Fox when at last they stopped the sled. "The presents are gone!"

"And look at my hat!" said Little Hedgehog. "What are we going to do?"

But just then, Badger
came wobbling down
the hill toward them.
"I followed the red wool,"
he chuckled. "I knew it
was from your hat,
Little Hedgehog!"

"You've found
Santa's presents!
Oh, thank you,
Badger!" said Little
Hedgehog. "But I'll never
deliver them in time for
Christmas now!"
"I'm sure you will,"
smiled Badger, "if we
all help!"

The friends dashed
through the
snow . . .

delivering
presents to
homes near
and far . . .

and high
and low . . .

working busily
through the
night.

The sky was turning pale blue and gold
by the time they had finished.
"Hooray!" cheered Little Hedgehog. "We did it!
Thank you, everyone. Santa will be so pleased!"

"What an adventure I've had!" sighed Little Hedgehog as he walked home. "I will miss my favorite red hat, though!"

But as he opened his door, he found a surprise . . . .

It was a present with a note:

For my wonderful Christmas helper.
Thank you! Love, Santa.

Inside was a brand-new hat—
hedgehog size!
"It's perfect!" cried Little Hedgehog.
"Thank you, Santa! What a special
Christmas this has been!"

For my wonderful
Christmas helper.
Thank you!
Love, Santa.